S0-AZK-853

The Japanese Americans

JENNIFER M. CONTINO

South Huntington Pub. Lib.
145 Pidgeon Hill Rd.
Huntington Sta., N.Y. 11746

MAJOR AMERICAN IMMIGRATION

MASON CREST PUBLISHERS • PHILADELPHIA

Japan is one of the most densely populated nations in the world. Here, pedestrians enjoy the scenery in Ritsurin Park, a famous park on the Japanese island of Shikoku.

The Japanese
Americans

JENNIFER M. CONTINO

MAJOR AMERICAN IMMIGRATION

MASON CREST PUBLISHERS • PHILADELPHIA

J 325.252
Contino

Mason Crest Publishers
370 Reed Road
Broomall PA 19008
www.masoncrest.com

Copyright © 2009 by Mason Crest Publishers. All rights reserved.
Printed and bound in Malaysia.

First printing

1 3 5 7 9 8 6 4 2

Library of Congress Cataloging-in-Publication Data

Contino, Jennifer M.
   The Japanese Americans / Jennifer M. Contino.
      p. cm. — (Major American immigration)
   Includes index.
   ISBN 978-1-4222-0610-2 (hardcover)
   ISBN 978-1-4222-0677-5 (pbk.)
   1. Japanese Americans—History—Juvenile literature. 2. Japanese
Americans—Social conditions—Juvenile literature. 3. Immigrants—
United States—History—Juvenile literature. 4. Japan—Emigration
and immigration—History—Juvenile literature. 5. United States—
Emigration and immigration—History—Juvenile literature. I. Title.
   E184.J3C673 2008
   973'.04956—dc22
                                                      2008026021

Table of Contents

MAJOR AMERICAN IMMIGRATION

America's Ethnic Heritage

Barry Moreno, librarian

Statue of Liberty/

Ellis Island National Monument

Ethnic diversity is one of the most striking characteristics of the American identity. In the United States the Bureau of the Census officially recognizes 122 different ethnic groups. North America's population had grown by leaps and bounds, starting with the American Indian tribes and nations—the continent's original people—and increasing with the arrival of the European colonial migrants who came to these shores during the 16th and 17th centuries. Since then, millions of immigrants have come to America from every corner of the world.

But the passage of generations and the great distance of America from the "Old World"—Europe, Africa, and Asia—has in some cases separated immigrant peoples from their roots. The struggle to succeed in America made it easy to forget past traditions. Further, the American spirit of freedom, individualism, and equality gave Americans a perspective quite different from the view of life shared by residents of the Old World.

Immigrants of the 19th and 20th centuries recognized this at once. Many tried to "Americanize" themselves by tossing away their peasant clothes and dressing American-style even before reaching their new homes in the cities or the countryside of America. It was not so easy to become part of America's culture, however. For many immigrants, learning English was quite a hurdle. In fact, most older immigrants clung to the old ways, preferring to speak their native languages and follow their familiar customs and traditions. This was easy to do when ethnic neighborhoods abounded in large North American cities like New York, Montreal, Philadelphia, Chicago, Toronto, Boston, Cleveland, St. Louis, New Orleans and San Francisco. In rural areas, farm families—many of them Scandinavian, German, or Czech—established their own tightly knit communities. Thus foreign languages and dialects, religious beliefs, Old World customs, and certain class distinctions flourished.

The most striking changes occurred among the children of immigrants, whose hopes and dreams were different from those of their parents. They began breaking away from the Old World customs, perhaps as a reaction to the embarrassment of being labeled "foreigner." They badly wanted to be Americans, and assimilated more easily than their parents and grandparents. They learned to speak English without a foreign accent, to dress and act like other Americans. The assimilation of the children of immigrants was encouraged by social contact—games, schools, jobs, and military service—which further broke down the barriers between immigrant groups and hastened the process of Americanization. Along the way, many family traditions were lost or abandoned.

Today, the pride that Americans have in their ethnic roots is one of the abiding strengths of both the United States and Canada. It shows that the theory which called America a "melting pot" of the world's people was never really true. The thought that a single "American" would emerge from the combination of these peoples has never happened, for Americans have grown more reluctant than ever before to forget the struggles of their ethnic forefathers. The growth of cultural studies and genealogical research indicates that Americans are anxious not to entirely lose this identity, whether it is English, French, Chinese, African, Mexican, or some other group. There is an interest in tracing back the family line as far as records or memory will take them. In a sense, this has made Americans a divided people; proud to be Americans, but proud also of their ethnic roots.

As a result, many Americans have welcomed a new identity, that of the hyphenated American. This unique description has grown in usage over the years and continues to grow as more Americans recognize the importance of family heritage. In the end, this is an appreciation of America's great cultural heritage and its richness of its variety.

This Buddhist temple stands in a garden in Kyoto, Japan. As an island nation, Japan was able to isolate itself from outside influences until the second half of the 19th century.

Japan Steps into the Modern Era

Unlike many countries, which consist of a large landmass, Japan is made up of nearly 3,000 islands. In the late 1800s, almost 50 million people lived in lands that, if combined, would be about equal to the size of the state of California.

Before people began *emigrating* from Japan to North America, the island nation had isolated itself from the rest of the world. For over 250 years, the leaders of Japan shut off the country to foreign trade and influence by closing its shipping ports so that ships from other nations could not enter Japan. The Edo government of Japan also made it against the law for people to read foreign books and learn about other religions, customs, or beliefs. The government did not want anyone or anything to challenge traditional Japanese values, such as obedience and harmony, especially within the family unit.

The family unit of Japan was also different from the rest of the world. Each family had a different role in society and belonged to one of four classes: samurai, artisans, farmers, and merchants. The highest class was made up of samurai warriors and government workers. The next class was made up of *artisans* and craftspeople—those who were skilled at making goods with their hands, such as statues, furniture, metal objects, or fine pottery. The third class was made up of peasants or farmers—those who grew food and owned land upon which crops or cattle were raised. The last and lowest class was made up of merchants and businesspeople—those who sold or traded goods and services that other people produced. In Japan, each person's role and class in society was decided when he or she was born, based on the job and class of the parents. There were no choices; children grew up knowing from the beginning what future job they would have.

Three Japanese samurai pose in armor with spears and knives in this colored print from 1860. The behavior of the samurai class was regulated by a code of conduct called Bushido, which means "way of the warrior."

Japan might have remained isolated even longer were it not for the United States Navy. In 1853, U.S. naval officer Commodore Matthew C. Perry arrived in Edo Harbor. He had a letter from U.S. president Millard Fillmore. The letter requested permission for American ships to stop at Japanese ports for supplies. The letter also suggested that it might benefit both countries to begin trading with one another.

In this colored 1890 photograph, a Japanese merchant carries two wicker baskets and several bundles of cloth using a wooden frame on his back. He supports himself on a walking stick. Before department stores and the Internet, traveling peddlers were an important way for country-dwellers to buy the things they needed.

Many Japanese did not want to trade or have any involvement with the Western world. Emperor Edo was afraid his country would be invaded, as Japan's neighbor China had been by the British. Japan had fought off numerous invaders before, but none of the invaders had the military might of the United States. Emperor Edo was also worried about the military strength of Great Britain and other European nations. He did not want to be invaded by any foreign power, so he agreed to develop trade relations with the rest of the world.

The people of Japan were angry with this decision. A rebellion occurred in Japan during the late 1850s that lasted until the late 1860s. After all the fighting was done, the leadership in Japan changed. The Edo emperor was *assassinated*; the capital city's name was changed from "Edo" to "Tokyo;" and a new family took power. A

15-year-old boy named Mutsuhito became the emperor of Japan. His reign, called the "Meiji Restoration," lasted from 1868 to 1912.

The Edo government had been run by the military, but the Meiji reign restored the power to one person, the emperor. The emperor had advisors who told him about policies and the outside world. They suggested that Japan become more modern and adopt features of the West. The advisors thought the best way to improve was to learn as much as possible about other nations. Therefore, the emperor allowed Japanese students to travel to the United States to learn about science, different forms of government, and the military. Some of these students were supposed to return to Japan and share their information with the emperor and his advisors so that Japan could grow and become more modern. The government paid for most students to study abroad, primarily at American universities such as Harvard, Yale, and Rutgers.

After the Tokugawa shogun was forced to abdicate in 1868, the young emperor Mutsuhito established the Meiji government. The name means "enlightened government." The year 1868 is regarded as the beginning of Japan's modern era.

It was also during the Meiji Restoration that most Japanese emigrants left for North America—in particular, Hawaii. The government wanted business, education, and the military to grow. In order for this to happen, expensive equipment, ships, and factories were needed. To pay for all those items, the government taxed the peasants heavily. The taxation destroyed many farm families because people just did not have the money to pay the huge tax. More than 300,000 families lost their land and belongings because they could not make the payment. As a result of the taxes and loss of income, Japan began to have problems keeping its residents from leaving the country.

Until 1867, it was against the law for people to leave Japan unless they were students or doing some other type of work for the government. However many had begun to secretly leave the country and become laborers on plantations or in factories. The Hawaiian Consul General in Japan hired some Japanese to work on Hawaiian plantations. German merchants also secretly took Japanese workers to silk farms in California. Since many people were sneaking out of the country, the Japanese government made it legal for other countries to *recruit* Japanese workers and for them to go to work in other countries. The government also opened its ports to visitors, and Americans began to travel to Japan. In 1868, the Japanese government passed a law that allowed its citizens to emigrate. Many left Japan for North America and the opportunities they believed would be found in that continent. ✷

Japanese children arrive in San Francisco, California, aboard the ocean liner *Shinyu Maru* in 1920. Unlike other immigrant groups that came to the United States and Canada, in general the Japanese did not become assimilated into American culture. In part, this was because most of the Japanese immigrants intended only to stay long enough to save some money, then return to their homeland. Another factor was the discrimination that many Asian immigrants faced in America.

2 The Journey to a New Life

Most people who thought about *immigrating* during the 19th century believed that there were economic and social opportunities in North America that were not available to them in their native lands. Japanese thought that in North America you could work and, in a few years, save enough money to live comfortably for the rest of your life back home in Japan. A majority of the Japanese immigrants were males between the ages of 15 and 39 who hoped to start a business, earn money, and then return home wealthy. The first generation of Japanese immigrants was called "Issei," a Japanese word that means "one."

A lot of the Japanese had never traveled from their country before and were relying on information posted in different guides to America. Many guides contained advertisements like this:

Come merchants! America is a veritable human paradise, the number-one mine in the world. Gold, silver, and gems are scattered on her streets. If you can figure out a way of picking them up, you'll become rich instantly to the tune of 10 million and be able to enjoy life. Come anyone skilled in the Japanese arts! You can earn a lot of money by making fans, ceramics, and lacquerware. Come students! Working during the day, you'll have time to attend night school in the evening.

Many found the thought of getting rich quick too hard to resist and decided to travel to North America, where they hoped to become successful and wealthy.

It was not easy to emigrate. The Japanese government screened potential emigrants at *quarantine*, or isolation, stations. Before an emigrant received a passport, he or she had to be tested for syphilis, hookworm, trachoma (an eye disease), and other illnesses. As many as 60 percent of the emigrants failed these tests and were not granted passports. American doctors examined most of the emigrants again before they were allowed into the United States.

After the decision was made to go to North America and a passport was granted, a long, slow, and hazardous journey lay ahead. Once aboard the ship, passengers could look forward to a trip across the Pacific that could last from two weeks to more than a month. The living conditions were nearly unbearable. Most of the Japanese did not get to travel in first class or even second or third class. Instead, the emigrating Japanese were boarded in the *steerage* compartments, which were about five feet high with two *tiers* of beds. Sometimes as many as 900 people were crowded together with room only for themselves and their belongings rolled up next to them. A narrow cot was provided for each person, but often it was not even wide enough to turn over on. Beds and bedding were not aired out or washed until the day before their arrival and inspection by the government officials. The only air and light available was through a hatchway, which was closed during stormy or rough

Japanese immigrants on their way to Hawaii aboard a steamship receive vaccinations against diseases. Hawaii, in the Pacific Ocean between Japan and North America, was a popular destination for Asians who wanted to start a new life. During the 19th century, immigrants from Japan and other Asian countries were encouraged to move to Hawaii because the island nation required laborers to work on its sugar plantations.

Once a rare delicacy, pineapple is a fruit now enjoyed in many parts of the world. These pineapple plantation workers in Lanai, Hawaii, are ensuring the quality of the fruit by checking the pineapples for defects as they are harvested. Many of the workers are descendants of immigrant laborers who arrived in Hawaii during the 19th century. Hawaii's population is more varied than that of any other state. Japanese Americans make up the second-largest racial group, after Caucasians.

weather. The air became increasingly filthy and foul as the journey progressed. There was never enough food and what little they did have was not cooked properly. Grain, hardened and served as a lump, was the common meal. Many Japanese brought their own rice and other dried foods because they were warned about the poor conditions on board. There was also a shortage of clean water and toilets for the number of passengers. The Japanese were not allowed to use the regular restrooms on the ship and had to use barrels with two boards across the top as their restrooms. The barrels were on the back deck of the ships with no privacy and long lines of people waiting for the chance to use them.

However, the thought of getting rich quick in North America made the journey bearable. Most of the first Japanese emigrants went to Hawaii to work on sugarcane plantations, where the pay was supposed to be high. On sugar plantations, the workers were promised a fair wage, so the Japanese government encouraged its citizens to go to Hawaii. Other immigrants found their way to West Coast states like California and Washington, where they worked as migrant workers, moving from farm to farm. Still others went to Mexico and Canada, where there were plenty of jobs as laborers, farmers, or migrant workers. ✺

Asian and Latino workers pause in a grape field during a grape harvest in California. Many immigrants were relegated to grueling physical labor and migrant work, often for meager pay.

3

Making a Living: Japanese Labor in Hawaii and the United States

The first Japanese immigrants in Hawaii worked mainly on sugarcane plantations. Once a laborer arrived on a plantation, he or she usually signed a contract that bound them to work for a period of time—usually three years. The contracts set the wages and amount of time a worker would stay at a particular job. Many were not used to the long hours and heavy labor involved with plantation work. The workday began at five o'clock in the morning and usually lasted 10 hours. There were no breaks or rest periods.

The work on the plantations was long and hard. Most of the new immigrants spent their time cutting sugarcane, hoeing the fields to get rid of weeds, and stripping the leaves from the sugarcane stalks. A few others worked in the steaming hot sugar mills where large, noisy machines crushed and pulped the sugar cane and boiled its juices into molasses and sugar.

Each worker had to wear an identification number on a brass tag. The workers were not called by name—they were called by their identification number. The bosses were cruel and whipped anyone not working fast enough. Workers were also **fined** if they accidentally broke a tool, were late, or did not produce enough. If a worker missed a day of work because he or she was sick, that person was made to work two days to make up for it. As if those working conditions were

JAPANESE EMIGRATION COMPANIES

Most Japanese workers were signed to contracts by Japanese emigration companies. These companies arranged for laborers to work in Hawaii and the United States. Many times, these companies lied to workers about pay rates, living conditions, and other benefits of working in North America.

After many negative incidents and reports of mistreatment of workers in North America, in 1894 the Japanese government issued regulations to protect the emigrants and make sure that the emigration companies did not lie to workers. The new rules set the hours of work, a fair pay amount, provided for money to be set aside for a return trip to Japan, and required the employer to protect and fairly treat each worker.

The Japanese emigration companies also had Japanese-speaking people and other Japanese immigrants who could speak English meet the new immigrants at the docks and take them to Japanese homes, where familiar food and conversation awaited, instead of leaving them to fend for themselves after leaving the boat. These new regulations and rules were supposed to help make the immigrants' life in North America better.

not bad enough, often one plantation would sell a worker's contract to another plantation and the worker would be sent to another place to live without any say in the matter. Many Japanese thought that system was unfair and cruel and no different from slavery. Furthermore, the Japanese were being paid less than Puerto Rican or Portuguese

Japanese-American fishermen use bamboo poles to pull in salmon off the coast of Maui, Hawaii. Fish has long been an important part of the Japanese diet. It is also an important part of Japan's economy, as the country's annual catch is 10 million tons of fish.

A group of Japanese-American farm laborers work in a field transplanting celery. Most of the Japanese immigrants who came to America during the late 19th century were industrious and ambitious.

workers. This angered many of the Issei. However, despite all these unfair conditions the Japanese worked hard for the plantation owners, and more and more immigrants began to settle in Hawaii. By 1900, the Japanese were the largest ethnic group in Hawaii.

In 1900, the Hawaiian Islands became a territory of the United States. The labor contract system that Hawaiian plantation owners were using was found to be illegal under U.S. law. The contracts that the Japanese immigrants signed were declared *void*, and 600,000 workers were now free to arrange their own work agreement. The Japanese began to organize labor unions to ensure fair pay and work hours. Some Issei also purchased land and began their own plantations. By 1914, Japanese farmers produced 80 percent of the coffee beans and 50 percent of the pineapples in Hawaii.

The hard work and skill of the Japanese in Hawaii was not limited to plantation work. Many of the Japanese immigrants also found work with the fishing industry. Some taught native Hawaiians tricks and techniques to help them catch more fish. Most of the large-scale fishing companies and processing plants in Hawaii were owned and operated by the Japanese immigrants. They also built boats and created other fishing equipment.

However, Hawaii was not the only place these new immigrants settled. Many made their homes in West Coast cities in the United States, and some made homes in Mexico and Canada.

The first Japanese man known to settle in Canada was Manzo Nagano, who arrived in British Columbia in 1877. Japanese immigrants did not begin arriving in large numbers in Canada until 1900. By 1914 there were about 10,000 Japanese immigrants in Canada. Most of these settled in the province of British Columbia, on the country's Pacific coast. However, laws made around this time limited Japanese immigration to Canada. In 1928, the laws were further revised to allow only 150 Japanese into Canada per year—a quota that was rarely met.

The population of Mexico had decreased during the second half of the 19th century, and skilled workers were needed to help the country modernize. Because there was a shortage of Mexican workers, companies started hiring Japanese immigrants to help with the labor shortage. The Japanese worked on farms, in mines, or in any other jobs that could help the Mexican economy grow. The number of Issei emigrating to Mexico increased after 1907. When a series of laws known as the "Gentlemen's Agreement" limited the number of immigrants who could enter the United States and Canada, many Japanese immigrants went to alternative locations, such as Mexico and other Latin American countries. ✹

THE GENTLEMEN'S AND LADIES' AGREEMENTS

Due to the large numbers of Japanese immigrants entering the United States, in 1908 the United States and Japan established an informal Gentlemen's Agreement, which limited the number of emigrating Japanese laborers. The Japanese government promised to only issue passports to merchants, students, diplomats, and tourists. Parents, wives, and children of laborers already living in the United States were also allowed to come and live with their families.

Japanese laborers who had passports for Mexico or Canada were denied admission to the United States after the Gentlemen's Agreement. Before the agreement, workers with passports to those North American destinations had been able to enter the United States without problems; now they would not be allowed.

Because the number of laborers was limited, more Japanese women began to emigrate to the United States. By 1909, after the Gentlemen's Agreement, the number of Japanese women immigrants outnumbered the males in Hawaii. The number of emigrating Japanese women was so great that in 1921, a Ladies' Agreement was issued to stop the number of female immigrants. However, by that time almost 20,000 Japanese women had come to the United States.

A Japanese-American family shares a toast of sake, a Japanese wine made from fermented rice. Many families have held onto their traditional heritage, while becoming assimilated into U.S. culture. The number of Asian Americans is growing rapidly, both in the United States and Canada. In 1960, there were fewer than 900,000 Asian Americans living in the United States; by 2000 that figure had surpassed 10 million.

4 Starting a Family in America

Japanese immigrants arriving in the mainland United States faced all sorts of problems. The teens who hoped to study in U.S. schools and universities often had to take jobs as domestic servants and go to school at night. Lots of white households hired these Japanese students as schoolboys and considered them ignorant and childlike. These teens, who were considered adults in their native land, were reduced to doing chores and assignments that were done primarily by women back home.

The students were not the only ones having problems. Some Japanese immigrants were tricked into signing labor contracts that did not pay or deliver what the worker was promised. Since few of the Japanese immigrants spoke English, they had to trust that the contract they signed was honest and fair. Most of the contracts and the people talking to the immigrants were not fair. However, by the time an Issei discovered the truth about the contract and work agreement, most were trapped in the jobs. Many worked in mining towns, logging camps, or railroad work gangs. Those jobs used English-speaking Japanese as bosses to supervise Issei laborers. Some bosses started their own companies and became labor contractors themselves.

Most of the first jobs that the Japanese immigrants took in the United States were as migrant farm workers. They lived in railroad

SCHOOLBOYS

During the 19th century, many teenage Japanese immigrant boys were able to get work in American homes as a "schoolboy." This term was used for a student-laborer who lived with an American family. In exchange for room, board, and sometimes a small payment, the boy would do jobs like cooking, washing dishes, chopping firewood, tidying rooms, and any other chores that were left for him.

A typical weekday for a schoolboy would begin at dawn. He'd get up before the rest of the family and start a fire, boil water, and set the table for breakfast. Sometimes he'd prepare the meal. After breakfast, he'd clear the table and wash the dishes. Then he'd attend school until 3:00 or 4:00 P.M. After school, he'd help make supper, set the table, then do the dishes, and study schoolwork for the rest of the evening. On Saturdays, he had extra house-cleaning duties that lasted the whole day. Sundays were his day off.

Many Japanese were ashamed to be schoolboys. Most considered the work to be for girls or women, and were upset that they had to do the jobs that were usually done by lower-class women in Japan. Many of the American families would not or could not pronounce the schoolboy by his proper name, so many were given American names like "Charlie," "Frank," or "Joe."

The purpose of a job like schoolboy was so that the teen could attend school, graduate, and get a better job. However, as time passed fewer and fewer schoolboys were able to attend good schools.

cars and moved from place to place. They got jobs helping to harvest crops and then moved on to the next farm. However, many wanted to own their own land and become farmers. There were four ways an immigrant could become a farmer. One was to make a deal with a landowner to agree to plant, care for, and harvest a crop in return for a set amount of money. This was a cheap way to farm because the landowner usually provided the seeds and equipment. An immigrant could also be a sharecropper. This way, a farmer paid part of the cost of operating the farm. He received a share of the profits when the crop was sold, instead of a fee. Another way to become a farmer was to rent the land. This way the farmer would keep all the profits after the rent and expenses were paid. Finally, a Japanese immigrant could purchase the farmland outright.

Some Japanese lost all their belongings when crops failed, but many more became successful farmers. Japanese farmers often led the way in agricultural advances and helped others learn how to grow crops. A lot of the land the Issei purchased was barren, dry land that most believed could not be farmed. Yet, the Japanese were able to turn that land into productive soil. By 1918, Japanese farm workers produced almost all of the California strawberries, asparagus, celery, and tomatoes.

Many Californians were jealous of the success that the Japanese experienced. Their feelings of jealousy were an important motivation behind the Alien Land Act, which was passed by the California State Legislature in 1913. The Act prohibited "aliens ineligible for citizenship"

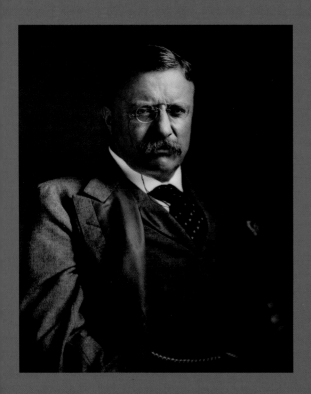

After Japanese schoolchildren were segregated from white children in San Francisco, the resulting protests from Japan led Theodore Roosevelt to make the "Gentlemen's Agreement" with Japan in 1908. Japan stopped issuing passports to laborers headed for America. This act slowed Japanese immigration to the United States for several decades.

from purchasing land or leasing it for a period longer than three years. Many Japanese were able to get around this law by purchasing land in the name of their children, who, if they had been born in the United States, were citizens and able to own land.

The people of other West Coast cities were angry and *biased* against the Japanese immigrants. The Issei faced lots of racial prejudice in the early years of the 20th century. People were worried that the number of Japanese immigrating to the United States would soon make the Asian population a majority in some cities. They urged the president to do something about the large number of Japanese entering the country.

In 1908, President Theodore Roosevelt made a Gentlemen's Agreement with the Japanese government. This agreement strongly encouraged Japan to stop issuing passports to laborers bound for the United States. Students and merchants could still get passports, but the workers were no longer issued passports. However, the Gentlemen's Agreement did not stop immigration because it had a loophole: wives or other close family members of men who were already living in the United States were allowed to immigrate.

Before 1908, the majority of Japanese residents in the United States were men. After 1908, many Japanese women began immigrating to the United States. There were three types of women who came to the United States from Japan. The first group consisted of brides of workers, merchants, and businessmen already living in the U.S. They were able to join their husbands if the husband had money saved in the bank and a good job. The second were women who married Japanese men visiting Japan from the United States in search of a wife. Those men were eager to settle permanently in the United States and begin raising a

Third-generation Japanese Americans call themselves *Sansei*. *Yonsei* are fourth-generation Japanese Americans. Fifth-generation Japanese Americans are called *Gosei*.

family. The last group of women who arrived in the U.S. were "picture brides." A Japanese man in the U.S. seeking a wife would have his picture taken. Then, the picture would be sent back to his family in Japan, and his family would show it to other Japanese families with unmarried daughters. The families would then decide if the man looked right for their daughter. If the man was acceptable, the daughter's picture was mailed to him. If both the man and woman were happy, the couple would be married in a Buddhist ceremony— even though the husband was thousands of miles away. The bride would travel by ship to the United States with his picture and look for him on the docks when she arrived.

Many Japanese were anxious to lead a normal family life in the United States and wanted to have their family around them. The children of Issei, the **Nisei**, faced many kinds of prejudice. They were **segregated** and forced to go to schools with other Asian children. They were teased because many did not speak English well. Anytime something was missing or a crime was committed, the police often investigated Issei and Nisei to see if they were involved.

Japanese people tended to gather together in the same area to live. These areas were nicknamed "Japantown," much like the Chinese section of any city was called "Chinatown." There was not a lot of interaction with their white neighbors. Japanese immigrants and their children wanted to be a part of the United States, but did not feel welcome. ✸

Members of a Congressional Committee inspect the passports of Asian "picture brides" at the Angel Island Immigration Station in California. Japanese-American men wishing to start families sometimes used family and friends to help them establish relationships with Japanese women, and the groom was often not present at the wedding ceremony.

The Asian community in San Francisco and other California cities is so prominent that certain sections of the city contain shops, businesses, and restaurants that cater to the needs of ethnic culture. Japantown in San Francisco is a huge social center for Japanese Americans.

5 Working Toward Acceptance

Japanese emigration to the United States nearly came to a halt during the 1920s. In 1921, several anti-Japanese land laws were passed in California and Washington. Those laws were followed by policies that excluded the Japanese from immigrating to the United States. On May 21, 1921, a law was passed that put limitations on the number of immigrants who could enter the United States from different countries. Japanese was one of the ethnic backgrounds singled out for exclusion.

Some of the Issei were worried that the policies to stop immigration, as well as the bad feelings some white people had toward them, meant that Japanese immigrants would never be welcome in the United States. As a result of the *prejudice* and *discrimination* that immigrants faced on a daily basis, the Issei and Nisei created another economy and culture besides that of their white American counterparts. The Japantowns thrived. Japanese Americans were successful as small businessmen and farmers. In 1925, almost half of the employed Issei in California were farmers or farm workers. They sold produce in Los Angeles, Sacramento, Fresno, and San Francisco. The Issei were loyal to the Japanese-owned stores, and many sent their children to Japanese-run segregated schools. The Japanese Americans only married other Japanese. The Issei and Nisei did not go into non-Japanese businesses, clubs, or schools.

A lot of the Japanese Americans missed Japan. Some planned on returning to visit; others planned to return to live. Many Issei felt that whites would never accept them and, for that reason, did not want to end their relationship with their birth country. In fact, some Issei did not believe in the American education system and sent their children to Japan for schooling. Those children were called *Kibei*, a term that meant "American-born but Japanese-educated." The Nisei who were not schooled in Japan still received a quality education; the Issei were determined to provide their children with the best schools they could. Many sacrificed their own needs in order for their children to have something better.

The Nisei were different from most children because they lived in two worlds. They knew the Japanese legend of the Peach Boy, a child who was found inside a peach by a childless Japanese couple and grew to be a great warrior but returned to take care of his loving parents; but they also were quite familiar with such Western stories as Cinderella, Little Red Riding Hood, and The Three Little Pigs. The Nisei were involved with Japanese dances and customs. They celebrated the birthday of the Japanese emperor but also liked to celebrate Christmas and New Year's Day. They knew the Pledge of Allegiance. Many Nisei "Americanized" their names: Danieru became Dan; Isamu became Sam. Most considered themselves half American, but that still did not change the negative view that most whites had of them. Only a small percent of the Nisei college graduates in the 1920s and 1930s could find work in the field for which they had a degree.

Anti-Japanese sentiment ran high in America during the 1920s. A resident of Hollywood, California, points to the anti-Japanese signs she has posted on her home.

Many white businesses would not employ the Nisei. Those who did get jobs with their degrees usually had only Japanese Americans as their patrons. Many were forced to take jobs that they had no training in, like gardening. The Nisei were kept on the outside, and many became angry at the poor treatment they received.

The Nisei wanted to fight against racism and prejudice, so they organized many clubs and organizations to protect their rights. One of these was the Japanese American Citizens League (JACL), a civil rights group that fought to ensure that no immigrants' rights were violated and that all people were treated fairly. The Nisei also organized Democratic clubs throughout California and other areas to support legal changes in government. Many were also active in labor union movements throughout the 1930s.

INSTRUCTIONS
1. Signup for JACL Members.
2. Check Birth & Marriage Certi
3. Get Cards.
4. Go to Typist.
   et Name Block.
   ngerprint.
   Card Certified by Boa
   Picture.

TOSHIE HORI
STUDENT

To avoid complications with civil and military authorities, these members of the Japanese American Citizen's League are receiving registration cards that certify them as U.S. citizens. The league, known as the JACL, was formed to protect Japanese immigrants from legal and vigilante harassment.

THE JAPANESE AMERICAN CITIZENS LEAGUE

The Japanese American Citizens League (JACL) was founded in 1929 to address issues of discrimination against the Issei and Nisei in the United States. In California, where the majority of Japanese Americans lived, there were many laws that limited the rights of Japanese. The JACL was established to fight primarily for the civil rights of Japanese Americans but also for the benefit of other immigrants. Although it was a small, California-based organization, the JACL was one of only a few organizations in the 1920s and 1930s willing to challenge the racist policies of the state and federal governments.

The true test of the JACL came in the 1940s when Japan attacked the U.S. Naval base at Pearl Harbor and launched America into World War II. After the attack, the FBI went to all Japanese communities in the West Coast and arrested any elders identified as leaders. The JACL was now in the difficult position of having to confront a hostile U.S. government whose intent was to exclude and imprison the entire Japanese-American population.

During the war, the JACL continued its efforts to ensure some measure of protection and comfort for Japanese Americans imprisoned in government detention camps. The organization argued for and won the right of Japanese Americans to serve in the U.S. military, resulting in the creation of a segregated unit, the famous 442nd Regimental Combat Team, which joined with the 100th Battalion from Hawaii and became the most highly decorated unit in U.S. military history, despite having only served in combat for a little over a year in the European theater of the war.

The day after the Japanese attack on Pearl Harbor, a Japanese-American storekeeper displayed this message in his window. The events of December 7, 1941, changed life for Japanese immigrants in the United States for decades.

6 Internment Camps and their Shameful Legacy

On December 7, 1941, Japan's Imperial Navy attacked the U.S. Pacific Fleet at a naval base in Pearl Harbor, Hawaii. More than 2,300 Americans were killed, and many ships and airplanes were destroyed. This action prompted the United States to declare war on Japan. This event also affected the Issei and Nisei living in the United States.

Newspapers and radio shows helped to fuel anti-Asian—especially anti-Japanese—feelings in the mainland United States. Many newspapers and other media had already warned Americans about the "Yellow Peril"—the term they had coined to call the Japanese living in the United States, many of whom had become successful farmers, laborers, and businessmen. Within hours of the bombing of Pearl Harbor, members of the Federal Bureau of Investigation (FBI) arrested many prominent members of Japanese-American communities along the West Coast. Ministers, businesspeople, reporters, teachers, farmers, fishermen, judo instructors, florists, restaurant owners, and others were removed from their homes along with their families. The Issei and Nisei were not told where they were going or when they would be returning.

A few months later, on February 12, 1942, President Roosevelt issued Executive Order 9066. Under this order, Japanese people living in the United States (Issei) and people of Japanese ancestry (Nisei and their children, known as Sansei) were removed from their homes and placed in internment camps without a trial or hearing. Their property and businesses were sold or seized, and most of their belongings were also removed. The Issei and Nisei were given notice on April 1, 1942, from the Western Defense Command and Fourth Army Wartime Civil Control Administration that "all Japanese persons both alien and non-alien will be evacuated from the designated area by noon on April 7, 1942." This gave the Issei less than a week to get their belongings in order and their property secured. Most sold their homes and belongings for a fraction of what the property was worth. Some tried to get friends to look after their homes and businesses, but many were unable to do so.

Many Americans insisted that the Japanese Americans were guilty of **_sabotage_**, even though there was no evidence to prove that any acts of **_treason_** had been committed. Americans thought that Japanese living near railroad tracks and airports were conspiring against the United States and helping the Japanese forces in the war effort. In order to prove their loyalty, many Japanese Americans joined the military and helped to staff and run the bases on the Hawaiian mainlands. Others volunteered for the armed services and offered to serve as translators and interpreters. They deciphered secret codes, giving the military vital information about Japanese battle plans. However, their efforts did not end the internment of other Japanese.

When the designated time came, the Japanese were tagged with identification numbers and then shipped to assembly centers, such as the Santa Anita racetrack. At Santa Anita, the Issei and Nisei were forced to live in horse stalls until they could be loaded onto trains and taken to another destination. Soldiers guarded the trains with weapons, and the blinds were drawn on each car so that the Issei and Nisei did not know where they were going.

Members of a Japanese-American family await relocation to an internment camp shortly after the United States entered World War II against Japan and Germany. Many Japanese-Americans lost their jobs and homes in the rushed relocation process.

Most of the internment camps were quickly built on Indian reservations of swamp and desert wastelands—areas that were not being used for anything productive and that were far enough away from other civilians so they would not see what the government was doing. Those areas were extremely hot in the daytime and terribly cold at night. One or two families lived in a single room made up of

A group of Japanese-American soldiers from the 100th Battalion. Many Japanese Americans served in the U.S. military during World War II, mostly in combat operations in Europe.

tarpaper without running water or privacy. There were public restrooms that everyone shared. There was not adequate medical care for the Issei or Nisei. The food was served in large *mess halls*. The men and women who worked while in the internment camps were paid next to nothing. Many only received $12 to $19 for a month's work, less than one-tenth what they had received when they were free. Armed guards and barbed wire fences surrounded the facilities. Anyone, including the elderly or small children, who wandered too close to the fence risked being shot or disciplined.

As the war raged on in Europe, the United States government wanted to know how the Japanese Americans really felt about Japan. All of the prisoners in the camps over the age of 17 were asked to fill out Loyalty Questionnaires. Many were worried they would be **drafted** based on their answers to the questions; even more were worried that when the war was over they would not have a country to live in. Any of the Japanese who answered "no" to the question of "Will you **foreswear** allegiance to the Japanese Emperor Hirohito?" were shipped to Tule Lake, an internment camp guarded by a full battalion of 920 armed guards and six tanks.

Many Issei and Nisei protested being held in these camps, and riots broke out in several of them. Some prisoners were killed for protesting against the conditions in which they were forced to live. Some were killed by accident. In 1944 at Tule Lake, a guard killed a man. The guard was fined $1 for using U.S. property—the single bullet—without permission.

On September 2, 1945, Japan surrendered and World War II was officially over. Many Nisei renounced their American citizenship and returned to Japan. On March 20, 1946, the last Japanese Americans left the internment camps and were given $20 and a ride back to their former homes. Most of the homes had been burned or destroyed. Some of the Japanese had become sick while in the camps and died. Others suffered nervous breakdowns or heart conditions and were ill for some time. Few people were able to leave the camps and return to the life they had before.

All the original struggles and problems the Issei faced were renewed, and now they and their children had to start over again.

In the years following World War II, many laws that allowed discrimination on the basis of race were changed. Many of the changes were due to the efforts and hard work of the JACL, which had worked hard to remind Americans about the contributions of Japanese Americans during World War II. The JACL reminded them of the Nisei 100th Battalion and the 442nd Regiment, which were made up of Hawaiian and mainland Nisei. They fought in Italy and France with great distinction. Members of the 442nd were awarded more than 18,000 individual medals for outstanding service in the line of duty. The JACL made sure that this was promoted in newspapers and other areas so that the anti-Asian laws could be changed.

In the 1950s, the Alien Land Law was revoked and the Japanese Americans were now able to own their homes and farms. In 1950, the McCarran-Walter Act allowed non-white immigrants to become citizens. Elderly Issei studied hard to be able to pass the test and become citizens of the United States.

Many Japanese Americans were ashamed of the fact that they were interned in camps. Even though their internment was not their fault, they still felt guilty. Some felt unsafe revealing the fact that they were Japanese to other races so they moved to different communities, tried to blend in, and ignored their own culture so that no one would realize their heritage. Some Issei were afraid that they would never be a part of or even welcome in the United States again. Others were determined not

INTERNMENT CAMPS

Following the Japanese attack on Pearl Harbor on December 7, 1941, President Franklin Roosevelt issued Executive Order 9066, which permitted the military to violate the constitutional rights of American citizens in the name of national defense.

Under this executive order, the U.S. military gathered Japanese Americans and persons of Japanese ancestry and placed them in internment camps. Over 120,000 people, half of whom were children and most of whom were U.S. citizens or legal permanent resident aliens, were imprisoned in these camps for up to four years without a trial or any evidence proving they were spies or traitors to the United States. Most were kept in the camps until after World War II was over in 1945.

In Canada, tens of thousands of Japanese citizens were ordered from their homes in British Columbia and dispersed through the country. They were forced to register with the government, and in many cases their property was taken away.

Almost 50 years later, the U.S. Congress passed the Civil Liberties Act of 1988, also called the Japanese-American Redress Bill, which acknowledged that a grave injustice was done to the Japanese Americans. This law mandated Congress to pay each victim of U.S. internment $20,000 in reparations. The reparations were sent with a signed apology from the president of the United States on behalf of the American people. That same year, Canadian Prime Minister Brian Mulroney made an official apology to Japanese Canadians and the government made reparations payments to these victims.

A group of schoolchildren in San Francisco—many of them Japanese American—recite the pledge of allegiance, circa 1942. After the end of the Second World War, Japanese Americans became more integrated into U.S. society.

to hide their heritage or the fact that they were angry at the treatment received in internment camps.

After World War II, the Japantowns on the West Coast disappeared. The Issei and Nisei who were interned did not want to return to their former homes. Many left the West Coast and settled in states across the U. S. Some Japantowns began in interior U. S. states, but most Japanese Americans moved away to mainstream communities as soon as possible after the war. Many Japanese Americans only traveled to Japantowns to shop, worship, or go to special events.

As the years went on, the Japantowns died out. With almost no new Japanese immigrants arriving, the need for Japantowns—and their subsequent growth—ended. In every U. S. city, except on the West Coast and in Hawaii, Japantowns disappeared. Like other ethnic groups, the Japanese Americans became more and more a part of U. S. culture. However, unlike most other ethnic groups, it was because they had been forced to. The internment camps of World War II left a legacy of shame and fear that compelled Japanese Americans to assimilate into American culture.

According to the 2006 American Community Survey, a project of the U.S. Census Bureau, today more than 1.2 million Americans claim Japanese descent. Canada's Bureau of Statistics, which oversees that country's census, estimates that more than 200,000 Canadians are descended from Japanese immigrants.

Immigrants from Asia, such as the Japanese, faced more racism and discrimination than any other ethnic group that came to America. Despite this, Japanese Americans have forged successful new lives for themselves in both the United States and Canada. Now that we have entered the 21st century, the contributions of Japanese Americans are only expected to increase. ✵

Famous Japanese Americans

Jun Atsushi He is the award-winning writer of the children's books *Crow Boy, Umbrella,* and *Seashore Story.* (All were published under his pseudonym, Taro Yashima.)

Brian Clay In the 2008 Olympics, he won the gold medal in the decathalon.

Leo Esaki Winner of the 1973 Nobel Prize for Physics for his work on electron tunneling theories.

Daniel K. Inouye A recipient of the Medal of Honor for his service during World War II, Inouye became the first Japanese American to serve in the U.S. House of Representatives (1959-1963) as well as the first in the U.S Senate (1963-present).

Daniel K. Inouye

Harvey Itano He won the Reverend Dr. Martin Luther King Medical Achievement Award for his outstanding contributions to research on sickle cell anemia, a disease that targets African Americans.

Pat Morita He played Arnold on the television show *Happy Days* and was in *The Karate Kid* series of films. He also made numerous television and commercial appearances.

Ellison Onizuka He was the first Asian-American astronaut. He was a member of the ill-fated space shuttle *Challenger* that exploded in 1986.

Stan Sakai He is the award-winning comic book creator of "Usagi Yojimbo."

Eric K. Shinseki He is the first Japanese American to achieve the rank of four-star general in the U.S. Army. He ended his career with a four-year term (1999-2003) as the army's Chief of Staff, the highest-ranking officer in the service.

Ronald Takaki A historian, Takaki's books focus on the experiences of immigrant groups in America.

George Takei He played Sulu in the *Star Trek* series on television and in films.

Kristi Yamaguchi She is a champion figure skater who won an Olympic gold medal in 1992.

Sandra Yamate She is an attorney, the founder of a multicultural children's book publishing company, and author of *Ashok by Any Other Name* and *Char Siu Bad Boy.*

Apolo Anton Ohno He competed for the U.S. team in the Winter Olympics in 2002 and 2006, winning five Olympic medals (two gold) in short-track speed skating.

Lindsey Yamasaki In 2002, she became the first Japanese-American player in the WNBA.

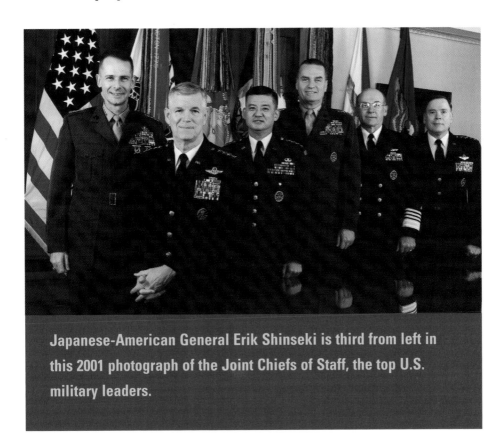

Japanese-American General Erik Shinseki is third from left in this 2001 photograph of the Joint Chiefs of Staff, the top U.S. military leaders.

Glossary

Artisans craftspeople who specialize in making a particular item.

Assassinate to murder by sudden or secret attack.

Biased having a definite opinion on someone or something.

Discrimination treating people different because of their differences.

Drafted to select a person for military service.

Emigrate to leave one's country of origin and go to another country to live there permanently.

Fine to make a person pay a fee as punishment for something.

Forswear to reject or renounce under oath.

Immigrate to come into another country from one's country of origin.

Mess hall the military term for the place where people eat.

Nisei the children of the Issei; the second generation of the Japanese immigrants.

Prejudice a preconceived judgment or opinion .

Quarantine isolate from normal relations or communication.

Recruit to secure the services of someone.

Sabotage a destructive action carried on by a civilian or enemy agent to hinder a nation's war effort.

Segregate to separate into groups on the basis of race, ethnic group, and so on.

Steerage a section in a ship with the worst accommodations, usually for the passengers paying the lowest fares.

Tier two or more levels arranged one above the other.

Treason the attempt to overthrow the government to which one owes allegiance.

Void of no legal force or effect.

Further Reading

Cieslik, Thomas, et al, editors. *Immigration: A Documentary and Reference Guide*. Westport, Conn.: Greenhaven Press, 2008.

Deneberg, Barry. *The Journal of Ben Uchida: Citizen 13559 Mirror Lake Internment Camp*. New York: Scholastic Paperbacks, 1999.

Kudlinski, Kathleen V., and Ronald Himler. *Pearl Harbor is Burning!: A Story of World War II*. Newark: Puffins Publishing, 1993.

O'Donnell, Liam. *U.S. Immigration*. Mankato, Minn.: Capstone Press, 2008.

Salisbury, Graham. *Under The Blood Red Sun*. New York: Yearling Books, 1995.

Sone, Monica Itoi and Frank S. Miyamoto. *Nisei Daughter*. Seattle: University of Washington Press, 1979.

Takaki, Ronald. *Strangers from a Different Shore: A History of Asian Americans*. Boston: Little, Brown and Co., 1989.

Tamura, Linda and Roger Daniels. *The Hood River Issei: An Oral History of Japanese Settlers in Oregon's Hood River Valley*. Champaign: University of Illinois Press, 1993.

Tunnel, Michael O. and George W. Chilcoat. *The Children of Topaz: The Story of a Japanese-American Internment Camp* Based on a Classroom Diary. Holiday House, 1996.

Uchida, Yoshiko. *Desert Exile: The Uprooting of a Japanese-American Family*. Seattle: University of Washington Press, 1984.

Byers, Paula K., ed. *Asian American Genealogical Sourcebook*. Detroit: Gale Research, 1995.

Carmack, Sharon DeBartolo. *A Genealogist's Guide to Discovering Your Immigrant and Ethnic Ancestors*. Cincinnati: Betterway Books, 2000.

Kawaguchi, Gary. *Tracing Our Japanese Roots*. Santa Fe: John Muir Publications, 1995.

Internet Resources

http://www.census.gov

The official Web site of the U.S. Bureau of the Census contains information about the most recent census taken in 2000.

http://www12.statcan.ca/english/census/index.cfm

The Web site for Canada's Bureau of Statistics, which includes population information updated for the most recent census in May 2006.

http://www.nikkeiheritage.org/

This is the Japanese Immigrants Heritage Web site, dedicated to the preservation, promotion and spread of information relating to the history and culture of Japanese Americans.

http://jcch.com/

The official Web site of the Japanese Cultural Center of Hawaii, a non-profit organization seeking to preserve and promote the evolving history and culture of Japanese Americans.

http://www.asianamericans.com/JapaneseImmigration.htm

A Web site dedicated to Asian Americans, with a detailed history of Japanese immigrants.

http://www.janm.org/

The official Web site of the Japanese American National Museum, preserving, promoting and educating the history, traditions and culture of the Nikkei.

Immigration Figures

Japanese Immigrants Obtaining U.S. Citizenship, by decade

1860-69:	**138**
1870-79:	**193**
1880-89:	**1,583**
1890-99:	**13,998**
1900-09:	**139,712**
1910-19:	**77,125**
1920-29:	**42,057**
1930-39:	**2,683**
1940-49:	**1,557**
1950-59:	**40,651**
1960-69:	**40,956**
1970-79:	**49,392**
1980-89:	**44,150**
1990-99:	**66,582**
2000-07	**68,824**

Source: Yearbook of Immigration Statistics, 2007.

Publisher's Note: The Web sites listed on the opposite page were active at the time of publication. The publisher is not responsible for Web sites that have changed their address or discontinued operation since the date of publication. The publisher reviews and updates the Web sites each time the book is reprinted.

Index

Photo Credits

Page

2: Corbis Images

10: Corbis Images

12: Hulton/Archive

13: Michael Maslan Historic Photographs/Corbis

14: Hulton/Archive

16: Bettmann/Corbis

19: Corbis

20: Michael S. Yamashita/Corbis

22: Michael S. Yamashita/Corbis

25: Stephanie Maze/Corbis

26: Library of Congress

30: Hulton/Archive

34: Hulton/Archive

37: Bettmann/Corbis

38: Joseph Sohm; ChromoSohm Inc./Corbis

41: Bettmann/Corbis

42: Bettmann/Corbis

44: National Archives

47: National Archives

48: The Mariners' Museum/Corbis

52: Library of Congres

54: Office of Senator Daniel K. Inouye

55: U.S. Department of Defense

Contributors

Barry Moreno has been librarian and historian at the Ellis Island Immigration Museum and the Statue of Liberty National Monument since 1988. He is the author of *The Statue of Liberty Encyclopedia*, which was published by Simon & Schuster in October 2000. He is a native of Los Angeles, California. After graduation from California State University at Los Angeles, where he earned a degree in history, he joined the National Park Service as a seasonal park ranger at the Statue of Liberty; he eventually became the monument's librarian. In his spare time, Barry enjoys reading, writing, and studying foreign languages and grammar. His biography has been included in *Who's Who Among Hispanic Americans*, *The Directory of National Park Service Historians*, *Who's Who in America*, and *The Directory of American Scholars*.

Jennifer M. Contino is a freelance writer for several magazines, including *Sequential Tart*, *Wizard*, *Comicology*, and *In Power*. She has a teaching degree in elementary education and also works with abused children as a mental health worker. Currently, she's working on a few children's books and a comic book set in Japan during the 1950s called "Divine Destiny."

AUG 2 6 2009

22⁹⁵